"…a potent vision of a winter interlude as seen through the eyes of Gray Wolf."
—*Booklist*, starred review

"With sparse, poetic text a drama unfolds."
—*American Bookseller*, "Pick of the Lists"

Winner of the ABC Children's Booksellers Choices Award
Winner of the Children's Council Science and Nature Book Award

Listen carefully and you will hear the wild, untamed music of Gray Wolf as he races along icy ridges, howls at the moon, fiercely defends his territory and, finally, finds a mate.

Readers will be entranced by the simple, poetic text, which follows the restless Gray Wolf as he wanders through a winter night, while the spectacular illustrations, by one of Alaska's premier wildlife artists, magnificently portray the grace and dignity of the noble wolf. For readers moved to learn more, a list of organizations is included at the back of the book, along with an informative note from the author and reader's guide that provide more detailed information on this elusive animal.

The Eyes of Gray Wolf offers an innovative approach to nature books and a dramatic look at a beautiful endangered species.

To Mrs McCulloch's Kindergarten —
HOWL!
Jonathan London
2010

THE EYES OF GRAY WOLF

For the wolves.

With thanks to Paula Wiseman and Victoria Rock,
and to Barry Lopez, who walked there before me. —J. L.

To Tex, Diane, Tom and Sasha … dedicated friends of the wolf. —J. V. Z.

First paperback edition published in 2004 by Chronicle Books LLC.

Text © 1993 by Jonathan London.
Illustrations © 1993 by Jon Van Zyle.
Reader's guide © 1994 by Marilyn Carpenter.

Book design by Carrie Leeb.
The illustrations in this book were rendered in acrylic on masonite board.
Manufactured in Hong Kong.

Library of Congress Cataloging-in-Publication Data
London, Jonathan, 1947 -
The eyes of Gray Wolf / by Jonathan London; illustrated by Jon Van Zyle.
p. cm.
ISBN-10: 0-8118-4141-3 ISBN-13: 978-0-8118-4141-2
1. Wolves—Juvenile fiction.
[1. Wolves—Fiction.] I. Van Zyle, Jon, ill. II. Title.
PZ10.3.L8534Ey   1993
[E]—dc20   92-35987
CIP
AC

10 9 8 7 6 5 4

Chronicle Books LLC
680 Second Street, San Francisco, California 94107

www.chroniclekids.com

THE EYES OF GRAY WOLF

by Jonathan London

illustrated by Jon Van Zyle

chronicle books · san francisco

As the full moon rises in the winter sky,
Gray Wolf goes hunting. He is restless.
He has lost his mate to a man's steel trap.

The northern night is cold and still.
Gray Wolf floats over the snow, drifting
through the woods, flowing like water.

He pauses only to inspect a scent mark,
or to claim his territory with his own scent.
He paws among rocks, where a year ago
he had hidden some meat—raided long since
by eagles, weasels, or wolverines.

Gray Wolf leaps a frozen creek and
climbs along the spine of a low ridge.

At the top, he closes his eyes, throws back his head, and howls. A wild, untamed music, it seems to bounce off the moon, echoing from the mountains and filling the gullies and valleys.

Nose into the wind, he returns to the hunt. In a moon-bright forest clearing, he flushes a snowshoe hare.

Shadows bound across the sparkling snow.
Hare is no match for Gray Wolf.

But Gray Wolf comes to a halt, letting Hare
flee. He sniffs the crisp night air, sensing
danger. The fur on his neck stands up.
There in the shadows he sees a wolf pack.

Poised, absolutely still, Gray Wolf stands alone and stares. His eyes burn like steady flames.

The leader of the pack stares back. Their eyes lock. The moon burns a hole in the night.

Suddenly a young white wolf, brilliant as the moonlight, steps out from the pack.

And the pack, still as stone,
watches as Gray Wolf and
White Wolf circle each other.
Even the trees seem to
hold their breath.

At the edge of the meadow they begin,
at the exact same moment, to wag
their tails and lope off across the snow,
their heads held high. The trees breathe
as the two wolves rise into the hills.

When they curl up together,
White Wolf buries her nose beneath
her bushy tail and goes to sleep.
But Gray Wolf's eyes remain open.
It has been a long night.
The moon has crossed the sky.
As it sinks in the west, the eyes
of Gray Wolf become twin moons.

In the spring the two wolves will start a new pack of their own.

What You Can Do To Help

There are many groups working to preserve the majestic wolf and to reintroduce wolves into their native habitats. If you would like more information, or if you would like to help, you can contact any one of the following organizations.

DEFENDERS OF WILDLIFE
National Headquarters
1130 17th Street, N.W.
Washington, D.C. 20030
(202) 682-9400
www.defenders.org

H.O.W.L. (Help Our Wolves Live)
www.helpourwolveslive.com

INTERNATIONAL WOLF CENTER
1396 Highway 169
Ely, MN 55731-8129
(218) 365-4695
www.wolf.org

WOLF HAVEN INTERNATIONAL
3111 Offut Lake Road
Tenino, WA 98589
(306) 264-4695
www.wolfhaven.org

WOLF PARK
4012 East 800 North
Battle Ground, IN 47920
(765) 567-2265
www.wolfpark.org

WOLF RIDGE ENVIRONMENTAL
LEARNING CENTER
6282 Cranberry Road
Finland, MN 55603
(218) 353-7414
www.wolf-ridge.org

WOLF SONG OF ALASKA
P.O. Box 671670
Chugiak, AK 99567-1670
(907) 688-9653
www.wolfsongalaska.org

 The wolf's range in the 1700s

 The wolf's range today

A Note from the Author

The Lakota Sioux call the wolf *shunk-manitu tanka*: "the animal who looks like a dog, but is a powerful spirit." This wild ancestor of the dog is a master hunter, and traditionally the Lakota people, among other Northern Plains Indians, learned from the wolves how to hunt and how to survive the long, cold winters. A wolf pack is similar to a human family, usually with a mother and father wolf as leaders, followed by uncles and aunts, brothers and sisters. The mother and father, who generally mate for life, lead the hunt and defend the young from bears and their territory from other packs. The wolves hunt and play together and care for each other.

Long ago, the wild howls of wolves were heard all across the Northern Hemisphere, throughout Europe and northern Asia as well as all of North America. But in the last few hundred years, humans have declared war on wolves, fearing them instead of learning from them—and learning how to live with them. In reality, wolves tend to be shy and try to avoid people, yet since the Middle Ages wolves have been seen as terrifying and evil. In the late 19th and 20th centuries, an attempt was made in North America to systematically destroy them. During this time, wolves were brutally hunted and poisoned to the brink of extinction.

Today, in the United States, wolves are endangered in the lower 48 states, except for Minnesota, where they are threatened. Thousands still roam Alaska and Canada, and conservationists are trying to protect wolves wandering back across the border to their ancestral homes in Montana, Idaho and Washington. In Yellowstone National Park, gray wolves have been successfully introduced, and elsewhere in the United States there are similar plans for their return. In western Europe, wolves survive in small numbers in the mountainous regions of Spain, Greece, Portugal, Italy and Scandinavia, while in eastern Europe, Siberia and the rest of Asia, nobody knows how many wolves remain. If we listen carefully, will we again hear "the wild, untamed music" of the wolves? By learning about wolves and their environment, and supporting organizations and sanctuaries that seek to protect the wolves, the answer could be "yes."

A Chronicle Books Reader's Guide

A Guide to Using This Book

Whether you are reading alone or sharing *The Eyes of Gray Wolf* with a group or classroom, this reader's guide can help you learn and discover the many layers of this book.

Before Sharing the Book

Ask readers what they know about wolves. List their answers. Are they scary, dangerous, friendly? Then ask the readers to list what they would like to find out about wolves. Invite them to listen to the book as you read aloud.

Reading and Discussing the Book

1. Read the text aloud, giving the readers plenty of time to enjoy the paintings and ask questions.
2. Ask readers what they've learned about wolves through the story. Make a list of their discoveries. Invite the readers to write about or draw wolves in light of this new knowledge.
3. Discuss the importance of Gray Wolf and White Wolf starting a new pack in the spring. Discuss in what ways this family unit will be similar to the human family unit.

After Reading the Book

1. Read "What You Can Do to Help" and "A Note from the Author." Share and discuss the map of the wolves' range.
2. Encourage older readers to write to the organizations listed in the back of the book for more information about wolves.
3. Visit the library and borrow folktales that feature wolves, such as *Little Red Riding Hood* and *The Three Little Pigs*. Read them aloud and ask readers to compare wolves' fictionalized, human-like nature with their natural characteristics. With help from "A Note from the Author," discuss why wolves have been depicted as villains in folktales.
4. There are many theories about wolf howls, including the one that suggests they simply enjoy it. More likely howling is a means of communicating among pack members as well as warning intruders in the wolves' territory. Howling could also be a form of bonding, a family roll call when members are separated or a way to coax stragglers and young animals to keep up with a traveling pack. Just as each wolf has its own distinctive odor, each also has a unique voice other wolves can identify. Discuss other ways human beings communicate aside from language.

For more information: *Wild Dogs* © 1994 by Erwin A. Bauer (Chronicle Books LLC)

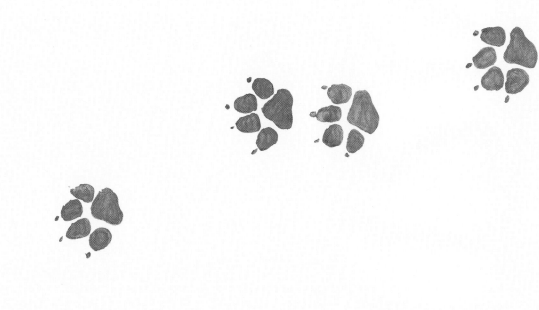

Jonathan London is the author of more than eighty books for children. He lives in Northern California with his wife, Maureen, and their sons. *The Eyes of Gray Wolf* is the first book in a series that reflects Mr. London's love and respect for the natural world.

Jon Van Zyle's art has garnered him numerous honors, including exhibitions with the Audubon Society and the Frye Art Museum. His prints, posters and lithographs are prized by collectors. He and his wife, Charlotte, live in Alaska, where they maintain a dog team of Siberian Huskies.

Also available
Baby Whale's Journey by Jonathan London, illustrated by Jon Van Zyle
"… a useful introduction to sperm whales." —*School Library Journal*

Honey Paw and Lightfoot by Jonathan London, illustrated by Jon Van Zyle
"… the book's implicit plea for wilderness preservation is eloquent."
—*Booklist*

Loon Lake by Jonathan London, illustrated by Susan Ford
"… satisfying read-aloud." —*Booklist*

Fire Race by Jonathan London, illustrated by Sylvia Long
"… a beautifully illustrated, carefully researched adaptation."
—*American Bookseller*, "Pick of the Lists"